BEWARE!!
DO NOT READ THIS
BOOK FROM
BEGINNING TO END!

Your little brother, Denny, runs off by himself in the huge Museum of Natural History building! You try to find him, but instead you discover the laboratory of the strange Dr Peebles.

The scientist "volunteers" you to test his new time machine! *Wow*, you think. *I'm going to be the first time-travelling kid ever!* Then Denny runs right into the machine—and vanishes!

Well, your brother's not lost in the museum any more. Now he's lost in time! You have to find him—again. But where? In the distant past, where fierce dinosaurs roam? Or in medieval times, battling with knights and wizards? Maybe in the future, where robots rule over humans! The one thing you know for sure is—*you must find Denny in two hours or he'll be lost for ever!*

You're in control of this scary adventure. You decide what will happen. And how terrifying the scare will be!

Start on page 1. Then follow the instructions at the bottom of each page. You make the choices.

SO TAKE A DEEP BREATH. CROSS YOUR FINGERS. AND TURN TO PAGE 1 NOW TO *GIVE YOURSELF GOOSEBUMPS!*

READER BEWARE—
YOU CHOOSE THE SCARE!

Look for more
GIVE YOURSELF GOOSEBUMPS adventures
from R.L. STINE

1 Escape from the Carnival of Horrors
3 Trapped in Bat Wing Hall

Tick Tock, You're Dead!

R.L. Stine

Scholastic Children's Books,
Commonwealth House, 1–19 New Oxford Street,
London WC1A 1NU, UK
a division of Scholastic Ltd
London ~ New York ~ Toronto ~ Sydney ~ Auckland

First published in the USA by Scholastic Inc., 1995
First published in the UK by Scholastic Ltd, 1996

ISBN 0 590 13894 4

Typeset by Rowland Phototypesetting Ltd
Bury St Edmunds, Suffolk
Printed by Cox & Wyman Ltd, Reading, Berks

10 9 8 7 6 5 4 3

What a crummy holiday!

You, your little brother Denny and your parents have come to New York City for the Christmas holidays. You thought you'd get to do a lot of cool things, like visit the Statue of Liberty, ride to the 102nd floor of the World Trade Centre, and ice-skate at the Rockefeller Centre.

Instead, your parents are museum freaks.

"It's entertaining," your mum says as she drags you into the Museum of Natural History.

"It's educational," your dad declares as he shows you a collection of ancient pottery.

"It's boring!" you say, but no one listens.

And the worst part is that you're supposed to be in charge of your little red-haired brother Denny. Only Denny doesn't want anyone to be in charge of him. "You're not the boss of me!" he keeps saying.

You follow your parents through the Museum of Natural History. At first it is sort of interesting. You really like the dinosaurs.

"Wait till you see what's in this room!" your mum cries.

Go to PAGE 2.

You rush to the next room, expecting something exciting. But your mum is standing in front of a sundial. "Isn't this wonderful?" she exclaims. "An exhibit on time!"

Great, you think. A whole roomful of clocks! Boring!

Then Denny gives you a karate kick in the back of the leg.

"Ow!" you cry. "Stop it!"

"You're not the boss of me!" he says smugly.

"Yes, I am!" you reply, punching him in the arm. He whines and complains to your parents. You can't win!

"I'm thirsty," Denny says now. You can see he's eaten almost half a bag of Gummi Bears in less than a minute.

"Can you find a drinking fountain for Denny, dear?" your mum asks without taking her eyes off a grandfather clock.

"Come on." You grab Denny's hand. But Denny pulls away and runs off down a hallway. You follow him. The hallway twists and turns. There's no sign of either Denny or a water fountain. But near the end of the hall you see a sign on a door:

WARNING!
DANGEROUS EXPERIMENT INSIDE
THIS DOOR MUST BE KEPT LOCKED AT ALL TIMES

Go on to PAGE 3.

Dangerous experiment? What does that mean? you wonder. You notice that the door is slightly open. Oh, no! Denny must have run in here, you think.

You push the door open wider and peek in. There's no sign of Denny. A tall, skinny man with long white hair tied in a ponytail is bent over a computer. The computer is hooked up to a big, strange-looking clock. Between the computer and the clock is a large square contraption that looks like a picture frame. You can hear the computer and the clock beeping and pinging.

"It's about time you got here!" the tall man says, straightening up. "I'm Dr Peebles. You must be the volunteer."

"Actually," you start to say, "I'm looking for—"

"There's no time to waste!" Dr Peebles interrupts. "I'm ready to start the experiment. Come on over."

"Well, I—"

"Here!" he says. He places a chain around your neck. On the end of the chain is something that looks like a stopwatch. A very, very odd stopwatch, with a complicated-looking dial and four big knobs.

"Are you ready?" Dr Peebles asks.

Turn to PAGE 4.

"Ready for what?" you ask.

"Why, to travel in time, of course," he replies. "You'll be the first human in history to use my travelling chronometer."

"Chronometer?" you echo. "What's that?"

He points to the stopwatch around your neck.

"I don't have time—" you start to say, but he interrupts again.

"Of course you have time!" Dr Peebles goes on. "It doesn't matter how long you remain in the past or future. When you return to the present, it will be the same moment that you left. It will be as if you weren't gone at all."

"How does this work?" you ask, pointing to the stopwatch.

"It's easy," says Dr Peebles. "Press the button on the left side to travel to the past. Press the button on the right for the future. To return to the present, press the top button and the bottom button at the same time."

Cool! you think. What if this guy's invention really works? Travelling in time would be awesome!

"There's no time to waste!" Dr Peebles says. "I'm ready to begin the experiment now."

Hurry to PAGE 5.

You think for a moment. Dr Peebles obviously believes you're someone else. But a trip through time sounds like a lot of fun. More fun than staring at crummy old bowls all day. And since you'll return at the exact same time you left, you'll still be able to find Denny and return to your parents before they know anything is wrong.

On the other hand, Denny can get into a lot of trouble very fast. And your parents will blame *you* if anything happens.

Make a decision now. Do you want to travel in time? Or should you look for your brother first?

If you choose to volunteer for Dr Peebles's experiment, turn to PAGE 71.

If you think you'd better stay and look for Denny, turn to PAGE 62.

"Use the key and open the lock!" the woman begs.

You hear the dragon's heavy footsteps approaching. "What key?" you ask.

"The key around your neck!"

You glance down at the chronometer. It seems to be the same shape as the keyhole. "But this isn't a key," you protest. "It's a chronometer!"

"I don't care what it is!" the woman cries. "Use it!"

At that moment flames shoot out of the opening in the wall. The dragon's huge, scaly face appears. Its evil yellow eyes narrow when it sees you.

Quick! Make a decision! Should you try to use the chronometer as a key to rescue the woman? Or should you just get out of there as fast as you can?

Hurry! The dragon's about to breathe fire again!

Use the chronometer on PAGE 94.
Run out of the room on PAGE 117.

KABBOOOM!

You zip out the bottom of the chute just as the plant blows up. A moment later you are surrounded by cheering rebels.

"You did it!" Jarmal slaps you on the back. "The war isn't over yet, but I am sure that we will win."

"Now help me find my brother," you say.

"I've located him on the space station," Jarmal tells you. "Some of the rebels sent him there for safety."

"I have to go there," you say.

Jarmal nods and leads you to a small space shuttle. "This will take you there," he tells you. "Good luck."

You say goodbye, then strap yourself into the automated ship.

Blast off to PAGE 98.

As the dragon moves nearer, you can feel the heat from its fiery breath.

What are you going to do?

It breathes fire again. Flames lick your feet.

"Dragon breath!" you hiss suddenly.

The dragon looks at you, startled.

"Dragon breath!" you say again.

This time it takes a few steps backward.

"Haven't you ever heard of mouthwash?" you say.

By now the dragon is hanging its head in shame.

You're not sure how much longer you can keep this up. But for now you've managed to stop yourself from meeting a fiery

END

"I choose school," you tell the judge.

The robot policeman drags you off to another room in the same building. You are surprised to see that it's a normal classroom with wooden desks, a blackboard and a computer centre. There is also a metal box the size of a cupboard standing in the front of the room.

The desks are all filled with human students about your age.

"We will continue the test now," the teacher says in a hollow voice. "Anita, what is the capital of Ulan Bator?"

A girl stands nervously. "I—I don't know," she stammers.

"Then you must enter the frammilizer," the teacher says.

The girl bites her fingernails as she goes to the front of the room. She climbs into the metal box. The teacher slams the door shut and presses a button. The box hums, then glows bright green. When the door springs open, you gasp out loud.

Turn to PAGE 36.

"The battle has started!" Jarmal shouts. "The domination of machines over people will end! Are you with us or against us?"

"Well, I—" Your words are drowned out by more explosions. The men and women around you have grabbed weapons and are racing down the tunnel.

"I'm against the robots!" you shout to Jarmal. "But I have to find my brother! If I don't get back to the present, we'll both be stuck somewhere in time."

"That's not my problem!" Jarmal snaps.

You turn away from him.

"We saw a child a day ago," Jarmal says in a softer tone. "Perhaps he was your brother. But he ran off and hid from us. I promise we'll help you find him—but only after you've joined us in fighting the robots. Do you agree—or not?"

Think it over carefully. You have only an hour till your time runs out. Can you trust Jarmal to help you find Denny? Or should you go back up to the streets now and look for Denny there?

To join the rebels, turn to PAGE 111.
To search for Denny now, go on to PAGE 37.

Denny loves dinosaurs. You decide to explore the swamp where you saw the dinosaur. You're sure Denny went that way.

As you move towards the swamp, tall, fern-like vegetation surrounds you. Your feet sink into the thick, mucky water.

Through the trees you can see huge shapes moving about. Real dinosaurs! Cool! you think. This is just like *Jurassic Park*—only better!

The dinosaurs are red, blue, green and lavender—as colourful as birds. Some dinosaurs are the size of dogs and cats. Other dinosaurs are bigger than a house. They're all munching on leaves and weeds.

You're about to move closer when a tremendous noise shakes the ground.

The trees sway as the rumbling grows louder. And louder. What's happening?

You peer through the giant ferns towards a grassy plain. Your eyes grow wide. You can't believe it. Lumbering towards you is—a *Tyrannosaurus rex*!

If you dare, go on to PAGE 65.

12

You reach into the pool of quicksand and feel around for the chronometer. Suddenly, the ground begins to shake violently. Under your feet the earth sways, and a deafening rumble fills the air.

"What's going on?" you yell to Denny. Smoke pours out of the top of a nearby mountain.

"A volcano!" you shout.

A second later, the top of the volcano blows off. Red-hot lava pours out. Even though the volcano is at least half a mile away, you can feel the heat against your skin.

Large rocks, glowing white-hot, begin to land in the swamp like bombs. "Watch out!" Denny shrieks. "Duck!"

You cover your head and throw yourself on the ground.

Whoomp! A rock just misses you. It splashes into the mud and throws up a shower of mud and water and—something shiny.

Could it be? Yes, it's the chronometer!

Quickly, you crawl over and scoop it up. It's covered with mud. Desperately, you feel for the buttons on the side of the chronometer. Your fingers close on two of them.

Press the buttons on PAGE 96.

You push the driver aside and manage to get your hand on the steering wheel.

You try to pull the lorry to the right, but it's much harder than you thought. The horrified faces of your family—including your own—loom in the windshield.

"GET OUT OF THE WAY!" you scream.

In desperation, you pull again on the wheel. With a sudden lurch, the lorry veers to the right.

You breathe a sigh of relief. You've done it! You've saved your family!

But you'd better hold on tight. You still can't stop the lorry. And this time the runaway vehicle is headed right at a brick wall! Stop reading right here. You don't really want to know what happens next. Let's just say you were a hit on Broadway.

THE END

You smile. You knew you could count on your brother's greed.

King Ruthbert orders the knight at your side to free your hands. You pull the chronometer off your neck. Glancing at it, you see that you and Denny only have five more minutes before disappearing in time.

"Denny," you tell him, "this is your last chance to return to the present. Please—"

"No!" Denny yells. "Forget it! I'm not going!"

"Give the boy the trinket!" the king bellows.

The knight beside you grabs for the chronometer. You whip your hands out of the way. The knight loses his balance and bumps you. You feel yourself falling off the platform— straight into the pot of boiling oil!

Go to PAGE 106.

"He's just an ordinary twentieth-century kid!" you protest.

"I'm not ordinary!" Denny yells. "I don't like this person," he adds, whining to the king.

"Listen to me, Denny!" you shout. "You're in big trouble. You've got to come with me now!"

"You're not the boss of me!" Denny yells.

"Boil this spy in oil!" shouts the king.

"Yeah!" Denny agrees, clapping. "Boil the spy in oil!"

"Denny, you're my *brother*!" you protest in horror. But Denny just smirks his obnoxious smirk.

Then the two knights grab you and begin to drag you out of the Throne Room.

"Wait!" you shout. "You're making a terrible mistake!"

But no one listens. You're dragged up to the roof of the castle. There, you see a bubbling black pot.

Yikes! Your hands are tied behind you. You can't use the chronometer. Unless a miracle happens, you're about to be boiled in oil!

Is this your lucky day?

If today's date is an ODD number, turn to PAGE 85.

If today's date is an EVEN number, turn to PAGE 52.

"I think my brother went to the future," you announce.

"I hope you're right." Dr Peebles punches another computer key. "Are you ready? Step through the Chronoport."

You enter the glowing frame. As you move through it you feel a strange tingling sensation.

"One more thing!" Dr Peebles calls out. His voice sounds far away. "Before you can return, remember—"

"What?" you cry as his words fade away. What was he saying?

Ahead of you in the mist are two scenes. One is a big, futuristic-looking city with small cars flying around like planes.

Another view seems to be of New York City. You recognize a few buildings, like the World Trade Centre and the Empire State Building. As you watch, a small red-haired boy who looks like Denny disappears behind another tall building. But is it really your brother?

Make a decision!

Is Denny in the strange city? If so, turn to PAGE 101.

Or is he the red-haired boy in New York? Find out on PAGE 54.

Denny shrugs and starts to explain. "I went through that door, and—"

But time is running out. You cut him off. "Stay here, okay?"

"You're not the boss of me!" Denny whines.

You groan. Your little brother is never going to cooperate unless you tell him the plan.

You whisper in his ear.

Denny gives you a big smile. "I'll stay around for *that*," he promises.

Read all about it on PAGE 53.

Herring Bros. is a big garage on the ground floor of a large, high-rise building. You step inside. There are just a few lorries. The only green one is easy to spot by the far wall.

In a booth by another wall, a woman with a microphone and headset sits behind a glass window. She's the dispatcher for the delivery firm. Maybe you can stop her from sending out the lorry. Or would it be better to talk to the lorry driver himself?

To speak to the dispatcher, turn to PAGE 20.
To talk to the driver, turn to PAGE 124.

You step up to the wizard's door, take a deep breath, and pull it open. Inside is a dim, smoky room. It's filled with a jumble of books, tables, pots of boiling liquid, crystal balls and other strange magical equipment.

"Hello!" you call. "Denny? Is anyone here?"

The only answer is a rustling sound behind you.

"Denny?" you shout, whirling around.

You gasp when you see what's there.

Crouched on a pile of rags behind the table is the biggest lizard you've ever seen. Around its neck is an iron collar with a name tag that reads . . . WIZARD!

A lizard named Wizard?

The lizard's cold black eyes gaze at you. Its narrow tongue flicks in and out. You take a step backward.

As the reptile starts toward you, you recognize the pile of rags it was sitting on—Denny's clothes!

You swallow hard. Now you know what happened to your brother . . .

And what will happen to you!

THE END

20

"Excuse me," you say to the dispatcher. "Can you help me?"

She slides open the glass window and says: "Here you are, finally! You're late."

She obviously thinks you're one of the shipping clerks. You are about to explain when she points to a red lorry. "You've got to load those crates right now," she says, adding, "Abe doesn't like to be kept waiting."

You look in the direction she's pointing and you see that the red lorry is parked right near the green lorry—the lorry you have to stop. Maybe this is your chance to delay the green lorry.

Quick—head over to PAGE 46. Abe doesn't like to be kept waiting.

As you look on in horror, your father sees the runaway lorry. He throws out his arms to hold back you, your mother and Denny.

Your family halts in their tracks ... and the lorry speeds on past!

You did it! You saved your family!

Now you've got to grab Denny and get back to Dr Peebles's lab.

"Come on, Denny," you call.

"No!" Denny cries. "You can't make me!"

You glance at the chronometer. Dr Peebles said you had to return within two hours of real time. The minutes are ticking by. You have to take Denny back as soon as possible, or you could get lost in time.

You're bigger and stronger—should you just grab him? Or can you talk him into going with you?

Grab Denny? Go to PAGE 122.
Talk him into it? Go to PAGE 134.

If only you'd taken swimming lessons when your mum wanted you to! You decide not to jump into the moat. You face the knight and his spear.

Right before he reaches you, the knight reins in his horse.

"Who are you, stranger?" he demands.

"I'm a visitor from the future. I'm searching for my brother."

"No one enters King Ruthbert's castle unless he can meet the challenge!" he replies.

"What challenge?" you ask.

"You must fight me, his Noble Defender, in a duel," the knight says with a smirk. "The loser will become food for the king's crocodiles in the moat."

Crocodiles in the moat? Good thing you didn't jump in after all!

The knight dismounts and pulls a bag of weapons from his saddle. You see a spear, a sword, a spiky chain, and a huge wooden club. "Here, you may choose your weapon," he says.

This guy really wants to have a *duel*?

"Well," the knight says impatiently. "Choose!"

Choose your weapon on PAGE 84.

"King who?" you ask.

"Do you take me for an idiot!" the knight snarls. "Henry's forces are expected to attack any day! Don't deny you're an advance scout!"

"I'm a kid from the future!" you repeat. "I only want—"

But the knight doesn't listen. He quickly ties your hands behind your back, then drags you up to the throne. He tosses you at the king's feet.

"Who is this?" the king demands.

"A spy for King Henry!" the knight answers.

You look up to deny it. That's when you notice who's sitting on the small throne next to the king.

Denny!

"I've been looking all over for you!" you tell him. "We've got to get back to Dr Peebles's lab! You can't stay—"

"Silence!" King Ruthbert bellows. "No one speaks to my son without permission!"

"Your son?" you gasp. "But this is my brother, Denny—"

"He's my son, Ruthelford!" the king interrupts. "I always wanted a son. When this boy appeared, I adopted him!"

Turn to PAGE 15.

Disguised in the uniform, you hurry out of the closet to explore the space station.

This place is too cool. Through the windows you can see thousands of stars. Sophisticated-looking computers with colourful lights are scattered all over this place.

The chronometer's steady ticking reminds you that time is running out. You'd better find Denny quickly and get back to the present.

You wander through a door and see a sign pointing to something called TELETIME.

Then two robots approach. One of them draws a laser.

Just ahead is a branch in the corridor. A green sign points to HYDROPONICS and a purple one points to ENGINE ROOM.

Make a choice and start running!

Follow the green sign to Hydroponics on PAGE 80.

Take the purple sign to the Engine Room on PAGE 74.

"I'm a new crew member," you lie to the captain. "I'm not a spy. I've been working in the Hydroponics area."

"Then why didn't you know the antigrav device is off limits?" she demands.

"I haven't finished reading the rule book," you say.

"Maybe so," the captain grumbles. She hesitates, then fires a question at you. "Are the crew quarters forward or aft?"

"Aft," you reply, hoping you're right.

"That's correct," she says. "But if you are a real crew member, what is the code for a space drill? A-Zero or X-Two?"

"A-Zero," you tell her.

"You are an imposter and a spy!" she shouts in triumph. "There is no space drill—and even the newest rookie knows it!" She turns to the robot guards at her side. "Shove this spy out through the airlock!" she orders.

"Hey—what about partial credit?" you yell. But it's no good. As you step out of the airlock, your whole body explodes.

Very messy. Very scary. Very much

THE END

"Excuse me, sir," you say, approaching the lorry driver. "The dispatcher said you might be able to help me," you explain. "My family and I are from out of town. I got separated from them earlier, and I'm wondering if you can give me a lift to my hotel."

"Sure thing, kid," he says. "Where is it?"

You give him the address, near the Museum of Natural History.

"That's right on my way," he says. "Come on, let's get started."

With a smile of relief, you follow him to the lorry and strap yourself into the passenger seat.

"How do you like the city, kid?" he asks as the lorry rolls along a broad avenue.

"It's great!" you tell him. "Lots of interesting—"

"Uh-oh!" the driver interrupts. "The accelerator!" he yells. "It's stuck!"

The lorry tears down the street. You glance back and forth from the driver to the crowded intersection straight ahead. You can see your family about to cross the street—and the lorry is gaining speed!

Race to PAGE 105.

"Wait!" you shout to the driver. "I've changed my mind!"

But it's too late. The driver can't hear you. With a lurch, the lorry starts off.

The lorry bumps along the city streets. Outside, you can hear honking horns and the engines of other lorries and cars. You're stuck back here with hundreds of dead fish—how are you going to save your family now?

You stand up and squeeze between the crates of fish. You make your way towards the driver's cab. You pound on the area behind the driver, trying to get his attention.

But the lorry keeps going.

And starts to pick up speed! It swerves wildly, and outside you can hear honking horns and angry shouting.

The lorry's out of control!

And you're stuck inside it!

It's too late to stop the lorry this time. All you can do now is press the button on the chronometer, return to the past, and try something else.

Return to the past on PAGE 31.

"The magical objects are three white stones," you tell the robot.

The robot's face is blank. "Correct," it says. "But we will see how you do in the next round."

You know you're never going to make it through the next round. You quickly grasp the chronometer and press the button on the right to go further into the future.

Immediately you feel a tingling sensation. When it stops, you're still seated—but not on the hard wooden chair in the classroom. Instead, you're strapped into a comfortable, soft seat. *Whoosh*ing sounds surround you.

Is this an aeroplane?

You glance out of a window. Outside is black, empty space, dotted with brilliant white stars. Up ahead is a big, doughnut-shaped structure with spaceships docked by its doors.

You're not on an aeroplane—you're on a space shuttle! And it's travelling towards a space station.

"Thirty seconds to docking!" an intercom squawks.

To find out what happens next, turn to PAGE 98.

You decide to try to trick the robot guards. You glance at the chronometer. Less than an hour left to find Denny and return to the present.

"When you get to the guards," Jarmal says, "tell them you have been sent to fix the romiframpton."

"What's that?" you ask.

"It's the central processor for the plant," Jarmal says. "Either the guard will believe you and let you through—or he will vaporize you on the spot."

Oh great, you think. No wonder no one else volunteered for this job. Jarmal gives you a pair of white coveralls to put on. You stick the red box in your pocket. "Good luck," he tells you.

You take a deep breath and approach the entrance to the power plant. A big metal robot with a laser gun stops you. "What do you want, human?" it demands.

"I'm here to fix the romiframpton," you say.

The robot hesitates. "We've received no report that it was broken." Your stomach lurches. Are you going to be vaporized?

Quick! Turn to PAGE 48.

30

The knight takes the club and holds it awkwardly.

This should be easy, you think as you pick an apple. You throw it to him—a fast pitch. To your surprise, he hits it—but the apple only flies a few feet.

"You'll never be able to beat that," the knight says.

"We'll see," you reply. He's never seen *you* play ball.

You grip the club tightly as the knight picks an apple. He winds up, then tosses it towards you.

You keep your eye fixed on the shiny red ball as it soars through the air. You shouldn't have any problem hitting this baby.

You reach back with your bat and start to swing. Then the bat connects—with empty air! You missed!

"Wait!" you cry. "Let me try again."

"Sorry," the knight says. "You can't change the rules."

"But—"

"The crocodiles are hungry." The knight picks you up in both his arms. "It's past their lunchtime!"

You start to reach for the chronometer. But it's too late. You're falling—falling into the moat. Below you are a dozen snapping jaws.

Too bad, batting champ! You've struck out big time!

THE END

You feel a strange tingling sensation as you press the buttons on the chronometer. When it stops you're still standing next to a newsstand. But a clock in a nearby shop shows that it's fifteen minutes before the accident.

You can still stop it from happening!

Your family has already started towards the corner.

You don't have much time! Should you do something to distract them? Or—just run across the street and warn them?

Think fast! The seconds are ticking by rapidly!

Distract your family on PAGE 40.
Warn them on PAGE 86.

You're sure that your brother is somewhere in the cave. "Denny!" you yell. "Denny!"

You're getting used to the smell and the darkness. You squint at the chronometer and see that there's only about fifteen minutes until you and Denny are lost in time for ever.

"Denny!" you call again.

At last you hear his faint answer. "Help me!" he calls. The sound is coming from underneath the straw.

You dig through the straw. Finally you find him, on the bottom, with ropes tied around his hands and feet.

"Who tied you up?" you ask as you quickly untie him.

"The lion," he says.

A lion tied him up?

"Come on," you say urgently. "Grab my hand. We've got to get back to the present!"

"You're not the boss of me!" Denny says. But you can see he's scared as he takes your hand.

You get ready to press the top and bottom buttons of the chronometer. But a terrifying roar fills the cave.

Find out what it is on PAGE 64.

"Come with me." The wizard leads you to a large room filled with dusty bookcases and magical equipment. He seats himself at a table and stares into a crystal ball.

"I'm thinking of a time-travel device," says the wizard. "It's a black cuckoo clock. A door in the centre of the clock contains a mechanical bird."

The wizard's green eyes seem to give off sparks.

"Here is the question: How do you make time run backwards? Do you pull the bird out of the door and put it back three times? Or do you twist its head around? Think carefully before you answer," he adds. "If you give a wrong answer you will be sent to the Corridors of Time—for ever."

If you've read the GOOSEBUMPS book *The Cuckoo Clock of Doom*, you know the correct answer. If you haven't read that book, you'll have to guess how to make time run backwards.

Do you pull the bird out and put it back three times? If so, turn to PAGE 60.

Or do you twist its head around? Turn to PAGE 82.

You've got to stop the lorry—that's the only way to save your family. Quickly you push the button on the chronometer. But a moment later you're on the same New York City street.

Uh-oh. Maybe the chronometer didn't work!

Then you notice a tall billboard with a digital clock and calendar. It's the same day, all right, but an hour earlier.

Whew. For now your family is safe. But you have to track down the lorry and make sure nothing happens.

You remember seeing HERRING BROS. DELIVERIES on the lorry's side panel. Quickly you look up the number and address in a phone book. Herring Bros. is only a few blocks away.

What are you waiting for? You only have an hour. Turn to PAGE 18.

You whirl around.

Whew! At least it's a human, and not a robot.

"Welcome to The City, stranger," the human says. "Who are you?"

"I'm a traveller from the past," you explain. "I'm looking for my brother."

"You won't find him here," the stranger replies. "It's not safe to be on the streets. Come with me."

"But who are you?" you stammer.

"Later!" he whispers. "We've got to hide!" He leads you to the corner, then down a manhole into an underground tunnel. It's dark, and you can hear water dripping all around you.

The tunnel leads to a large room lit with candles and lanterns. Several other humans are inside.

"Welcome to the rebel stronghold," says the man. "I'm Jarmal, leader of the rebellion."

Rebellion? What's this guy talking about?

Find out on PAGE 109.

The girl is gone!

"Jackson," the teacher goes on, as if nothing has happened. "What is 43,000,000 divided by 7.645328?"

A tall, pale boy stands up. He doesn't answer for a moment, then shakes his head. "I don't know," he says.

"Go into the frammilizer!" the robot commands.

Slowly, Jackson walks to the front of the room. He steps into the box. A moment later he, too, is gone. Frammilized.

You watch in horror as your classmates disappear, one by one. In a moment it will be your turn. You've got to do something and do it fast!

You could use the chronometer to leave the future, but you haven't found Denny!

On the other hand, you've always done well in school—maybe you'll be able to answer the teacher's question.

Answer the teacher's question on PAGE 133.
Use the chronometer on PAGE 68.

"I'm sorry," you tell Jarmal. "I hope the humans win over the robots. But I've got to go and look for my brother."

"That's bad news—for you," Jarmal says. "But it's good news for us. We've been looking for someone to use as bait to lure the robots into the underground tunnels."

"Wait a minute!" you say. "I've changed my mind! I want to join the rebel—"

"Sorry," Jarmal replies. "It's too late." He snatches the chronometer and crushes it beneath his boots.

"But I'm a fellow human!" you protest, as Jarmal and two other humans drag you back to the manhole.

"It makes no difference," Jarmal snarls. "If there's one thing five hundred years of robot rule has taught us, it's not to be sentimental."

The rebels tie you to the top of the manhole. Then Jarmal and his friends gather below, their guns drawn and ready. Outside on the street you can hear gunfire—and it's getting closer.

When the robots arrive, you'll be caught between the two opposing armies. Too bad. It looks as if you've become tied up in one adventure too many!

THE END

The high, wooden door to the castle stands open. "Hello?" you call. "Is anybody home?"

Your own voice echoes back. You step through the door into a dark entrance hall. Hanging from the wall is a tapestry. In the centre there's a picture of a fierce-looking beast.

A lion? you wonder. You sure hope you don't run into him here!

You enter a winding, narrow corridor. Empty suits of armour line the walls. The only light comes from flickering candles.

The corridor turns and twists, but doesn't seem to lead anywhere. You glance at the chronometer. Only one hour left—and there's still no sign of Denny!

Then all the candles go out.

You're in total darkness!

From somewhere up ahead, you hear an eerie scream. A human scream. Chills creep up your spine. Who was that? Maybe you should get out of here right now.

But what if it was Denny?

If you chose to go on, turn to PAGE 76.
If you decide to turn back, go to PAGE 51.

Terrified, you reach up to help your brother. Your hand brushes a thick, rope-like strand. You try to pull back in disgust, but your hand is stuck. You raise your other hand to help. And your other hand gets stuck, too!

"Denny!" you cry. "I'm trapped!"

"Here it comes!" Denny shrieks in terror.

The glowing red lights move slowly towards you. They're not lights—they're eyes ... the eyes of the gigantic spider that made the web.

And it's the biggest spider you've ever seen!

With huge, dripping fangs.

Frantically you struggle against the sticky strands, but it's no use. This time you've become totally wrapped up in your adventure!

THE END

What would make you and Denny turn around? you wonder. You've got to create a distraction.

You glance at the newsstand again, and an idea comes to you. It's not much—but it's the only thing you can think of.

Quickly, you check your pockets. You've got about thirty dollars—your allowance, plus some money your dad gave you to buy souvenirs.

You ask the newsstand owner for change. You get a handful of notes and coins. Suddenly a familiar-looking, red-haired boy runs past you. You stare at him, then glance back at your family. Denny is still with the rest of the family—what's he doing here, too?

"Denny!" you shout. "What are you doing here?"

Turn to PAGE 17.

"It's King Henry's army!" King Ruthbert shouts.

The king's two knights spring into action. They drop you and jump in front of the king. They desperately try to defend him against the invading army.

When the knights let you go, you roll out of the way. You've got to grab Denny and get out of here. Fast!

But one of King Henry's knights has already seized your brother. You watch in horror as the knight lifts your brother over his head and walks him over to the end of the castle.

Oh, no! The knight's about to toss Denny over the side!

You've got to do something, but what? For just a moment you think about doing nothing. After all, Denny was planning to have you boiled in oil. But no—he's your brother, after all.

Your hands are still tied behind your back. Maybe you can trick the knight into letting Denny go. Or—maybe you can roll into the knight's path before he reaches the edge of the roof.

Trick the knight on PAGE 121.
Roll into his path on PAGE 91.

You push open the door and step into the power room. You can feel the hot green glow from the power source on your skin. You place the red box next to the glowing orb and get ready to run.

Just as you reach the door, it slams shut!

Oh, no. It's locked!

Through a window you can see a robot guard on the other side. It's laughing at you!

Desperately you reach for the chronometer. But the device turns white-hot and start to melt in your hands! Somehow the pulsing glow is destroying it!

You push and pull on the door again, but it won't budge.

The explosive device is programmed to go off within one minute. That minute is nearly up. Maybe the rebels will be able to help—

BOOM!!!

Maybe not . . .

THE END

Frantically you pull the vine out of your path and race to the exit. The plant sends tendrils racing after you. They snap at your ankles.

A cluster of geraniums twists and turns towards you. As you approach, one of them sprays a bubbling pink solution at you. You skid in the slimy liquid and fall down.

Up ahead a giant cucumber plant hurls its fruit. You duck as a grapevine fires off hard green grapes.

HELP! You're being attacked by plants!

You scramble to your feet and barely make it to the exit. You fall into the corridor outside.

Take a deep breath and turn to PAGE 69.

"I'll look for my brother in the past," you tell Dr Peebles.

"Fine," the scientist replies. He punches another set of numbers into the computer.

"Now step right through the Chronoport," Dr Peebles instructs you. "And good luck."

You approach the shimmering frame and enter it. You feel a strange tingling sensation. Everything appears hazy, as if you are underwater. A second later you see two paths ahead in the mist.

Wow!

At the end of the left-hand path you squint to see a tall stone castle in the distance. A knight in shiny armour on a white horse rides towards it.

At the end of the right-hand path there's a swamp with tall, strange-looking trees towering over it. Moving among the trees is . . . can it be? A dinosaur!

Which path did your brother choose? Which one will you take? Quick, decide!

If you think Denny ran towards the knight, turn to PAGE 93.

If you think he investigated the dinosaur, turn to PAGE 11.

You step between the bookcases and find yourself in a small, dark cave filled with piles of straw. The air is damp and smells terrible.

In one corner there's a dent in the straw, as if a very large animal has been lying there. Next to the dent is a pile of bones with teeth marks in them.

"Denny?" you call nervously. "Denny, are you in here?"

"Help me!" A sudden, faint voice fills the cave. It's your brother. "Help me!" he cries again.

The voice seems to be coming from the back of the little cave. You crawl further back and see several piles of straw and a small opening. You press your eye up to the opening and peer inside. In the darkness, several tiny red lights glow.

"Help!" Denny's voice sounds fainter and more terrified.

But where is he? Is he hiding behind one of the piles of straw? Or did he go through the opening?

Make a decision quickly. Time is running out!

If you crawl through the opening with the red lights, turn to PAGE 92.

If you stay in the cave, go to PAGE 32.

46

You walk over to the loading area, hoping you'll be able to convince someone to stop the green lorry. But how?

"What are you doing daydreaming?" Abe bellows. He's a huge scary man. "Start loading, NOW."

You lift the first crate. It's heavy, but you manage to hoist it into the back of the lorry. That wasn't so bad—it's the next thirty or so that wear you out.

Your back is breaking, but every time you stop—even for a second—Abe is there saying "Load!" So you keep an eye on the green lorry as you load.

To your horror, you see the driver of the green lorry climbing into the front seat and getting ready to go. You've got to stop him! You start to run over to him, but Abe is coming around the corner. Can you get away from Abe? That's a matter of luck. Are you wearing something green today?

If you're wearing green, turn to PAGE 104.
If you're not, turn to PAGE 63.

"What?" you cry. You stare at the scientist. Your parents are going to ground you for life if you lose Denny.

"You'll have to travel in time to find him," Dr Peebles tells you. "I'd better make those adjustments to the Chronoport so you don't disappear into timelessness, too!"

You stare at the scientist as he fiddles with the time machine. You can't believe it—this guy is really serious!

"When you find your brother," Dr Peebles goes on, "you must be touching each other before you use the chronometer. Otherwise, the device will bring only one of you back."

"No problem," you say. "But where did Denny go? The future or the past?"

"There's no way to know whether he's gone forward in time—or back," Dr Peebles replies. "You'll have to guess."

You touch the chronometer around your neck. It began measuring real time the moment Denny disappeared. Already the seconds are ticking by. You have to decide: Are you more likely to find Denny in the past or in the future?

Travel to the future on PAGE 16.
Go to the past on PAGE 44.

48

The robot guard looks you up and down. You keep staring at his gun.

"The *romiframpton*," you repeat.

"Broken again?" the guard replies. "Go on in. You know where it is."

Actually, you *don't* have any idea where the romiframpton is. But you don't care. You're in!

A steel walkway leads straight ahead. Next to it, a ladder stretches up.

Which way is the power source?

Take the walkway on PAGE 118.
Climb the ladder on PAGE 128.

As soon as you place the red box against the wall, it begins ticking. Jarmal said you'd have one minute to escape from the power plant. That's not enough time to make it down the ladder! Then you spot a small door behind the ladder, labelled EMERGENCY EXIT.

You throw yourself towards the exit. You're in a slick chute that leads down. You slide towards the bottom, holding your breath. Will you make it before the plant blows?

Slide on to PAGE 7.

"Wait!" you cry. "You don't need to—" But it's too late. He's already jumped into the water. You watch in horror as the crocodiles swim towards him—jaws open!

"One last thing," the knight calls before the beasts reach him. "Beware of the Lair!"

"The what?" you ask. But the only answer is the snapping of the crocodiles' jaws.

Trying not to watch or listen, you hurry across the drawbridge and into the castle.

Turn to PAGE 38.

You decide to try to get out of this creepy castle. Using the wall to guide you through the darkness, you start back. You've only gone a few steps when you feel a doorknob with your fingers. You turn it and step into a smoky room filled with red light.

"Who's there?" calls a frightened-sounding woman. Before you can answer, she cries out, "Please help me!"

You make your way through the smoke towards the sound of her voice. At the back of the room, chained to the stone wall, is a beautiful blonde woman. She's dressed in a flowing green gown.

"Help me!" she screams. "Find the key and unlock the chains before he comes back!"

"Before who comes back?" you ask.

"The dragon!" she says. "He went into his den to take a nap. You've got to save me!"

Now you see an opening in the wall. Smoke is pouring out of it with a hissing sound. This must be the dragon's den. You look at the chain holding the woman to the wall. The lock is a very strange shape—nearly round.

"Hurry!" she shrieks. "I hear the dragon returning!"

Turn to PAGE 6—if you dare.

The two knights drag you over to the pot of boiling oil. The king and Denny are right behind them.

"On the count of three, carry out the sentence!" the king orders.

"Denny, help!" you plead.

But Denny sticks his tongue out at you. Then he gives the king the thumbs-up sign.

"One!" the king says. The knights pick you up.

"Please—just listen to me—" you cry.

"Two!" The knights lift you high in the air above the pot.

Frantically, you struggle to free your hands, so you can use the chronometer. But they are tied too tightly.

"Three—" the king cries. At that moment, a hair-curling scream splits the air. Dozens of armoured knights rush on to the roof. They're all waving swords and knives and holding out large shields. The roof is swarming with knights ready for battle!

Turn to PAGE 41.

You quickly jump up on the counter of the newsstand, and then climb on to the roof.

"Hey!" the owner shouts. "Get down from there!"

You ignore him. While he continues to yell, you take some of your money and throw it down on to the pavement. "FREE MONEY!" you shout.

Down below, Denny shouts the same thing. "FREE MONEY!"

"Look at that!" someone shouts. "Those kids are throwing away money!"

Two or three passers-by pick up coins and notes. A crowd starts to gather and cars and taxis brake to see what's going on.

You watch as Denny bends down and pockets some of the change.

"Denny!" you scream. "Put that—"

Loud honking starts up in the distance. The lorry is coming! You can see it now—speeding for the intersection where your family is about to cross!

Quick! Turn to PAGE 58.

54

You glide through the mist towards the New York City street where you saw the red-haired boy. Honking taxis, buses and lorries zip along the street. Tall buildings surround you. On the streets, people are shouting, arguing and laughing.

Uh-oh. This looks exactly like New York City in the *present*. Maybe something went wrong with the chronometer.

You glance around for the red-haired kid you saw. But you don't see him anywhere.

You approach a corner newsstand. "Excuse me," you say to the vendor. "Can you tell me how to get to the Museum of Natural History?"

"What do I look like, an information booth?" he snaps back at you.

"Never mind," you mutter. "Who needs your—"

Then you notice a stack of newspapers. The one on top has tomorrow's date. You're in the future all right—one crummy day in the future!

Not fair! you think. You're about to push the right-hand button on the chronometer to travel further into the future when something makes you gasp.

Find out what it is on PAGE 77.

You love the zoo! What a weird punishment, you think, as the police robot takes you away in a flying car.

Soon you zoom through the zoo gates. Giraffes, elephants, tigers and antelopes roam around the grounds. Instead of bars, a shimmering transparent force field separates the animals from the viewers.

"You will remain here," the robot announces, stopping in front of an exhibit that looks like a living room, with a couch, chairs and a TV.

The robot yanks the chronometer off your neck.

"Give that back!" you shout, but the robot ignores you. It aims its laser gun at the force field around the exhibit. The field dissolves, and the robot pushes you into the exhibit.

"Wait a minute!" you protest. "You can't leave me here!"

"I'm sure you will be comfortable," the robot tells you. It zaps its gun again, and the force field goes back up.

"No!" you cry, trying to push through the force field.

Then a group of robots approaches. Two little ones point and make strange coughing noises.

What are they pointing at?

Find out on PAGE 102.

56

You decide your best chance for escape—and for finding Denny—is to go to the past.

The teacher finishes questioning the girl in front of you. Before the robot gets to you, you press the left-hand button on the chronometer. You feel a tingling sensation, and the classroom disappears.

The next thing you know, you are standing on a familiar-looking pavement. Across the street, a robot strolls along, looking in shop windows.

Is this the past? This is the same spot where the robot policeman picked you up!

But it's nighttime now, you realize a minute later. You've travelled to the past, just not very far back.

You hear approaching footsteps and quickly duck into a doorway. You stay very, very still.

Then you feel a hand come down, hard, on your shoulder.

Turn to PAGE 35.

You step through the door labelled TO THE LAIR. You find yourself in a very narrow passageway. Smoking candles along the walls give off a little light as the path twists and turns. You're beginning to wonder if you made the wrong choice when you see something on the path.

A squashed Gummi Bear.

Your heart stops. There were no Gummi Bears in medieval times. Denny's been here!

You hurry along the corridor and see more squashed Gummi Bears. Your brother has definitely come this way. But where is he now?

You come to a narrow staircase. You follow the cold stone steps downward. At the bottom is a big, wooden door. Over it, a sign says LAIR OF THE WIZARD.

Next to that door is a tiny door about a foot high. The sign over the small door says LAIR OF THE LIZARD.

You think again about the knight's last words to you: "Beware of the Lair." But which lair did he mean?

Approach the Lair of the Wizard on PAGE 19.
Check out the Lair of the Lizard on PAGE 113.

58

You look over at your future family. The future Denny and the future you are laughing and pointing at the shower of money.

Your parents are watching, too. Then your father points to his watch and says something. The others nod and start for the corner again.

"No!" you shout.

A split second later, the green lorry hurtles towards the crowded intersection. Brakes squeal and horns blare. You freeze, barely able to watch the scene unfolding in front of you.

Your mother lets out a blood-chilling scream. Have you saved your family?

Find out on PAGE 21.

In just a moment you'll be safe in another part of the future.

"Stand and answer!" the robot demands, pointing at you.

You stand. You're holding the chronometer with your finger on the right-hand button.

"What," the robot asks, "is the quallicork of—"

You don't wait for the rest of the question. You press the button. You feel a tingling sensation, and the next instant . . .

You are still standing in the classroom and the robot is still speaking: "—on the right-hand adjubibble in Jupiter?"

You press the button again, but you're still in the same place. Is the chronometer broken?

You glance at the dial while you press again. Now you see with horror that it is taking you into the future—but only five seconds at a time!

Go to PAGE 73.

"Pull the bird out three times!" you cry.

"WRONG!" the wizard thunders. Instantly, there's a brilliant flash of light. You find yourself in a misty corridor. With a sinking feeling, you realize you are in the Corridors of Time.

In the distance you see an old man trudging along, with the help of a cane. You hurry to catch up. The man has a white beard and thinning grey hair. There's something familiar about him . . .

"Hi," the old man says in a creaky voice.

It's Denny! Somehow the Corridors of Time have turned him into an old man!

You grab his arm. "Denny," you say, "come on. Maybe we can find a way out of here."

He shakes off your hand. "You're not the boss of me," he grumbles. Then he bops you on the head with his cane. "I'm older now—and I'm the boss of you!"

Too bad. You're stuck in time with your older younger brother!

THE END

You take off after your brother. But by the time you reach the tree where you last saw him, he's gone.

Then something on the ground near the tree catches your eye. It's the chronometer. But where's Denny? And why did he leave the chronometer behind?

You scoop up the device and run your finger over the buttons. Denny said he wanted to do something else. He was probably bored with the past and decided to go to the future.

You quickly press the button on the right and feel a tingling sensation.

A purple mist surrounds you. Everything turns blurry. You close your eyes, hoping your dizziness will pass.

You open your eyes again. And blink. Twice.

A futuristic-looking city looms in the distance.

Enter the city on PAGE 101.

Are you serious? Would you *really* rather look for your brother than take a trip in time? Well, then, you're reading the wrong book! GOOSEBUMPS readers only have time for adventure.

Take a minute and think it over . . . then go back to page 5 to choose again!

Turn to PAGE 5.

You're heading over to the green lorry when you feel Abe's heavy hand on your back. "Get in," he says, shoving you into the back of the red lorry. "You've got to unload at the other end." He slams the door. You're locked in. There's no way you can help your family now.

You're squeezed in with all the boxes you loaded. Even though you loaded dozens of them, you never really looked at them. Some light is coming in from a crack in the roof, so you can make out the address on the boxes: BROOKDALE LABORATORY.

Then you notice that there are small holes in the boxes. You put your eye right up against one of the holes and you see an eye staring back at you!

Creepy.

Turn to PAGE 135.

64

A hideous lion stands at the entrance to the cave. It's enormous—bigger than any lion you've seen at the zoo. Its head is covered with yellow-brown fur and a thick mane. Its eyes glitter as it looks you up and down.

Then you recognize the beast.

It's the lion from the tapestry in the entrance-way to the castle!

In terror, Denny ducks behind you.

"You'll do just as well!" the creature snarls as it rushes towards you. It grabs you by the arm, licking its lips hungrily.

You glance at the chronometer in your hand. The lion is touching you, so if you press the chronometer buttons now it will travel to the future with you and Denny. But if you *don't* go to the present soon, you and Denny will be lost for ever.

Should you stay here? Or return to Dr Peebles's laboratory with both Denny and the lion?

To escape now, turn to PAGE 72.
To stay and fight the lion, turn to PAGE 95.

The huge tyrannosaur towers over the other dinosaurs. It's bigger than you ever imagined. Its teeth are as long and sharp as carving knives.

The enormous creature lets out a roar as it crosses the grassy plain. You freeze. Your heart pounds in terror.

The other dinosaurs all start to run away. But one, who was grazing on ferns, is slower than the others. The tyrannosaur easily catches it up, and tears off the small dinosaur's head in one bite!

Then the tyrannosaur swings its head and stares straight at you! You take off as fast as you can. The tyrannosaur follows. Closer and closer.

Ahead there's a swampy patch of land. You race towards it. Something small is sitting in the middle of the swamp.

It's Denny!

But what's he doing? Why isn't he moving?

You glance back over your shoulder. The dinosaur is still right behind you.

"Denny!" you call out. "Run!"

"I can't," he yells back. "I'm stuck in quicksand!"

Help your brother on PAGE 110.

66

A tingling sensation races through your body as you're transported back to the present and the Museum of Natural History. When the misty air clears, you're back in the time exhibit, standing near a sundial.

"Come on," you say to Denny, sighing with relief. "Let's go and find Mum and Dad."

"No way," two voices reply in stereo. "You're not the boss of me."

"Oh, no," you moan out loud as you realize what you've done.

Both Dennys have returned to the present with you!

You've saved your brother's life, but ruined your own.

THE END

You've got to hit the brakes. The lorry is speeding along even faster than before. You try to reach the brake pedal with your foot—but you can't reach!

With horror you watch as your family steps into the intersection. You dive down to the floor of the lorry. Using both hands, you push on the brake pedal as hard as you can.

SCREEEEEECH!!!!

Will it stop?

Turn to PAGE 97.

You get ready to make your escape from the classroom. You need to find your brother before his time runs out, but it's too dangerous to stay here.

Now the robot is questioning the girl sitting in front of you. While she stammers out an answer, you grasp the chronometer.

Where should you go? Do you think you might find Denny in a time further in the future? Or perhaps he's in the past? Maybe you should return to Dr Peebles's laboratory and ask his help in finding your brother.

Whatever you decide to do, choose now! The teacher is about to question *you*!

Return to the laboratory for Dr Peebles's help? Try PAGE 127.

Seek Denny further in the future? Go to PAGE 59.

Or look for him in the past? Turn to PAGE 56.

You lean against the wall of the corridor, trying to calm yourself. The only person who can help you find Denny is Dr Peebles. You pull the chronometer from under your uniform and press the top and bottom buttons to return to his laboratory. You've got to escape before anyone—or anything—comes after you again.

But nothing happens.

You press the buttons again, and nothing happens.

Oh, no.

What will you do now? You glance up and notice the sign pointing to TELETIME. Maybe it has something to do with time travel. Maybe there's another way to get back to the present.

Enter Teletime on PAGE 81.

As you back away from the vicious flower, its curling vine sends out new shoots.

Beyond the plant you see a sign marked EXIT. Can you get around the vine and make your escape?

Or, off to your right is a rack of garden tools. You see a long rake that looks pretty sharp. Maybe you'd better get the rake first and fight off the vine.

Quick! Make a decision! Will you grab the rake first? Or run straight for the door?

To grab the rake, turn to PAGE 123.

To try to go through the exit, turn to PAGE 43.

"I'm ready to travel through time!" you tell Dr Peebles.

"Good," the white-haired man replies. He punches some numbers into the computer keyboard. The computer starts to hum. The square doorway between the clock and the computer fills with a strange, shimmering glow. "The Chronoport is almost ready," the scientist says, pointing to the frame. "I only need to adjust—"

But before he can continue, you hear pounding footsteps. You turn to see Denny racing towards you.

"Denny!" you cry. He's heading straight for the Chronoport. "You can't go in there!"

"You're not the boss of me!" Denny yells. He runs straight through the glowing frame. There's a soft *pop* before he disappears completely.

"Oh, no!" Dr Peebles cries. "He went before I made the final settings! If you don't bring him back within two hours of real time, he'll disappear into timelessness for ever!"

Race on to PAGE 47.

You grab Denny's hand and press the chronometer buttons to escape.

Nothing happens.

"What's going on?" Denny whines, tugging at your arm.

"I don't know," you snap.

You let go of Denny's hand and stare closely at the face of the chronometer. It looks okay. Same as always. You wonder what went wrong.

Then the lion roars. Loudly!

You shake the chronometer up and down. And try pressing the buttons again. Your body starts to tingle.

It's working! you think. You shut your eyes tightly. Your fingertips tingle with what feels like an electric current.

You open your eyes. You can't believe it! You're not back in Dr Peebles's lab. You're still in the castle. In front of a door that says KING RUTHBERT'S THRONE ROOM.

The lion is gone. But where is Denny?

And then you remember—you didn't hold Denny's hand. You've lost him all over again! And time's running out!

To search for Denny again, go to PAGE 83.

Frantically you start to press the other button, for the past. The robot rolls over to your side. It grabs the chronometer away from you. "No playing with toys during class!" it shouts. "Now answer the question!"

You have no idea what quallicorks or adjubibbles are. And you don't think you'll have time to find out.

Too bad—but it looks as if the answer to your question this time is:

TIME'S UP

You follow the purple sign and rush into the Engine Room area. It's crammed with machinery and monitor screens. At the centre is a control panel with banks of blinking lights. Next to the control panel is a clear plastic chamber, about the size of a car, labelled ANTIGRAV.

Inside the chamber is a small figure that's floating and turning in mid-air.

It's Denny! You yank open the door. "Denny!" you call. "We've got to get back to the present right now!"

"I don't want to," he whines.

You step into the chamber, but your feet don't touch the floor. There's no gravity here—you're weightless! You get a funny feeling in your stomach as you start to float around.

You grab for your brother—but he easily twists away. You find yourself upside down. If you weren't so worried about returning to your own time, this would be fun. "Come on, Denny!" you beg.

"You're not the boss of me." He sneers at you.

You grab for him again—and miss. Then you glance outside the chamber—a robot guard has his laser gun pointed straight at you.

Turn to PAGE 115.

An instant later, you find yourself back in the laboratory at the Museum of Natural History.

"Welcome back." Dr Peebles looks relieved to see both you and Denny. "How was your trip?"

"Exciting," you say.

"Boring," Denny whines. He punches you. "I'm hungry!"

You gaze at your brother with exasperation. You know that if it weren't for you, he would have disappeared for ever. You think of everything you had to go through to save him. And for just a moment, you wonder if it was such a good idea.

THE END

The screams echo against the dark walls. You wish you could turn around and get out of here. But you have to find your brother.

"Denny?" you shout.

You put your hand on the walls to guide you. A light appears up ahead, and you follow it into a circular room.

Inside the room are three doors. You just came through one of them. The other two are labelled TO KING RUTHBERT'S THRONE ROOM and TO THE LAIR.

You remember that the knight warned you to "Beware of the Lair." Did he mean this lair?

What about the Throne Room? Judging by this spooky castle, that could be pretty dangerous, too.

Which door do you choose?

Enter the Throne Room on PAGE 83.
Step into the Lair on PAGE 57.

Strolling down the block in front of you is a familiar-looking family: a father, a mother and two kids. There's a very good reason why the family looks so familiar. It's *your* family.

You watch as your mum, dad, Denny and *you* continue down the block. Your parents are talking to each other, and you and Denny seem to be arguing—some things will never change.

You watch as Denny gives you a karate chop in the arm, and you punch him back.

It feels so strange to watch yourself like this. There are two of you in the same place! What would happen if you spoke to your future self?

You still haven't decided what to do when your family reaches the corner. The light changes and they start to cross to the other side of the street.

A moment later you hear frightened screams and shouts, and then loud honking. You turn towards the noise. A green lorry is speeding down the street.

The lorry shows no sign of slowing down, and it's headed straight towards your family!

Quick! Turn to PAGE 87.

"Yeah, get out of here!" Denny adds. A karate chop lands on your arm.

You can't help it. You punch him back. "Don't be a jerk!" you say. "Turn around now! If you don't something terrible will happen!"

"You're not the boss of me!" Denny yells. He rushes towards the intersection.

"Stop!" you yell again. Denny turns around and kicks you, hard, in the shin. You are so mad you grab him in a headlock. "Say you're sorry!" you yell.

"You're not the boss of me!" Denny screams again.

This time the other you jumps into the fight. While you hold on to Denny's neck, the you from the future pokes him in the chest.

"Say you're sorry," you demand, tightening your hold on his neck. "Say it."

This time you don't even see the lorry bearing down on you and your family. It's too much fun having two of you to gang up on Denny!

THE END

You decide to sneak in through the air duct. Jarmal leads you through the trees to the back of the power plant. The air duct is a small opening near ground level. Slipping the red box of explosives under your shirt, you climb into the opening. Then you begin to inch your way along the duct.

The duct is so small you can scarcely move. As you go further in, the space becomes even tighter. You crawl another foot—then realize you are stuck! You can't go forward, and you can't go back. And your hands are trapped at your sides.

You can't reach the explosives or the chronometer. You are about to yell for help when you hear shouting outside.

Whump!

Laser guns fire. The robots must have found the rebels!

"The small human is in the air duct, Commander!" a robot says. "We'll close the air duct so it can't breathe!"

CLANG!

The cover of the air duct bangs shut.

Looks like you've picked the wrong side in this battle, human. Sadly, your adventure has come to a breathtaking

END

80

You tear down the corridor to the Hydroponics area.

What a jungle! Thick, green leaves and winding vines creep all around the room. Strange-looking plants grow everywhere. You notice they're all potted in a pink solution that is bubbling furiously.

You watch the doorway as you look around. The robots may catch you up at any minute.

"Denny!" you call. "Are you in here?"

You wander past odd-shaped leaves, strange-smelling flowers, and heavy, colourful fruits. You've never seen anything like them. You wonder if something in outer space caused ordinary earth plants to mutate into strange new forms.

You come to a large sign that reads DANGER.

Huh? What could be dangerous in a room of plants?

Then you see it: a vine with a stem as thick as an elephant's leg. Its flower is huge, with sharp-looking petals.

You step forward for a closer look. Suddenly the flower lunges at you, its petals snapping shut an inch from your nose!

Back away on to PAGE 70.

You follow the sign to Teletime. It's a spacious room full of electronic equipment. A large panel in the centre of the room contains dozens of TV monitors.

On the monitors you can see several scenes from the past: Alexander the Great's army, the signing of the Declaration of Independence, the landing on the moon. A robot in a white lab coat watches the monitors and doesn't notice you.

Maybe the robot can help you return to your own time. You're about to ask for help when an alarm sounds.

"ATTENTION ALL PERSONNEL!" a loud-speaker squawks. "BE ON THE LOOKOUT FOR AN INTRUDER!"

The robot scientist whirls around and spots you. He pulls out a laser gun. "Explain yourself!"

What do you do now? Tell the truth and ask the robot for help? Or try to trick it?

Ask for help on PAGE 125.
Trick the robot on PAGE 99.

"I know the answer," you tell the wizard. "To make time run backwards, you have to twist the head of the cuckoo."

The wizard waves his arms. A moment later there is a brilliant flash of light and the wizard disappears. In his place stands Denny.

You never thought you'd be so glad to see your little brother.

"Denny!" you cry. "I've been looking all over for you!"

"I've been *hiding* from *you*!" he replies.

You glance at the chronometer. Now there's less than thirty minutes till your two hours are up. "Denny," you tell him, "we've got to go back to Dr Peebles's laboratory. We've got to go *now*—"

"You're not the boss of me!" he exclaims.

"Come on!" you insist. You reach for his hand, but he yanks it away.

"I don't want to go!" he cries. He runs into the mist and disappears at the back of the Lair.

Turn to PAGE 114.

You step through the door labelled TO KING RUTHBERT'S THRONE ROOM and climb a short flight of steps. At the top, you enter a huge stone room.

Colourful tapestries hang on the walls between narrow, arch-shaped windows. Ladies in long gowns sit on wooden benches. Around the room, knights in armour stand stiffly to attention.

At the far end of the room, a wooden throne stands on a raised platform. Sitting on the throne is a fat, bearded man wearing a red robe and gold crown.

King Ruthbert, you realize.

Next to him, on a smaller throne, is a small person. His crown is too big and slips down over his face.

A nearby knight draws his sword and raises it to your throat. The sword lightly pricks your skin.

"What are you doing here, stranger?" the knight demands.

"I'm a traveller from the future," you quickly explain. "I'm looking for my brother. He has red hair and—"

"Silence!" the knight shouts. "I'll not listen to any more of your lies! You're a spy for King Henry!"

Turn to PAGE 23.

84

As you reach for a weapon, you notice an apple tree planted alongside the moat. Suddenly you have an idea—and it's just what you need to put a chink in this knight's armour.

"I choose the club," you tell the knight. "But we'll duel according to my rules."

"Very well, stranger," the knight says. He hands you the club.

"See that apple tree?" you say. "Pick one of the apples and toss it towards me. I'll hit the apple with the club. Then I'll throw an apple for you to hit. Whoever hits the apple furthest will win the duel."

"A strange challenge indeed," the knight grumbles. "But I accept."

Last year you were the best batter on your baseball team. Now you're hoping your batting average will pay off. Can you beat the knight at baseball? To find out, flip two coins.

If both coins come up the same, heads or tails, turn to PAGE 30.

If one coin comes up heads and the other comes up tails, turn to PAGE 116.

The knights drag you to a platform above the pot of boiling oil. With a gulp you look down into the seething black fluid. In another second you'll be sizzling like fried chicken!

You twist your hands behind your back. But the ropes are too tight to break through.

The king and Denny climb up to the roof to watch.

"Do you have any last words, spy?" the king asks.

"Yes!" you say. "Please let me take Denny . . . er . . . your son away from here. If he stays he's doomed!"

"Never!" the king roars. "Prepare to carry out the sentence!"

"Denny!" you plead. "You can't let him do this! You've got to listen to me! Tell him not to do it!"

Hear Denny's reply on PAGE 132.

You've got to warn your family. "Stop!" you cry as you dash across the street. "Go back to the hotel!"

At first they all ignore you. Then your mum's eyes grow wide. She looks back and forth between you and the other you.

"I don't have time to explain what's happening!" you shout at her. "Don't cross the street! Mum, please! It's dangerous!"

But now your family is hurrying to get away from you. They're totally freaked out!

"Stop!" you cry again.

"I don't know who you are or why you're pretending to be my child," your father says angrily. "But if you don't leave us alone, I'm calling the police!"

"Please!" you beg. "Just stop for a minute! You have to listen to me! I'm trying to save your—"

"I mean it," your dad says. "Get out of here or you'll be sorry!"

Turn to PAGE 78.

The lorry picks up speed as it approaches the corner. There's no way your family can get out of the way.

In another moment they will be flattened like pancakes, and there's nothing you can do!

But maybe . . .

You touch the chronometer. Maybe you can go back in time and stop the accident before it happens.

Should you go back in the past a few minutes and try to stop your family? Or go back further in time and try to stop the lorry?

To stop your family, turn to PAGE 31.
To stop the lorry, turn to PAGE 34.

The knight uses his sharp sword to slash the ropes around your arms. You're free!

Before the knight can question you further, you jump up and karate kick the sword from his hand.

The sword falls to the ground. You can't believe the karate lessons you took last summer worked! You karate kick the knight again.

And lose your balance.

You reach out and grab Denny and tumble to the ground, hitting a button on the chronometer.

You sprawl on the ground, dizzy. And then you hear it. "All hail the king! All hail the king!"

You gaze up and gasp. You're in a strange land. And hundreds of people are chanting and bowing. Bowing to *you*!

You are the king!

You stand up and give your first order. "Take this slave boy away," you say, pointing to Denny. "I *am* the boss now."

THE END

You follow the robot into a big, glass-walled building. He leads you to a courtroom. A shiny robot dressed in black sits behind a tall desk.

The judge, you realize.

"You are accused of appearing in the streets, human," the judge says. "How do you plead?"

"Guilty, Your Honour," you say. "But I didn't—"

"Silence!" the judge cuts you off. "There are no excuses. For punishment, you may have your choice: You will be sentenced to school or to the zoo."

School? The zoo? What kind of punishment is this? To find out, make a choice now.

Get sentenced to school, turn to PAGE 9.
Go to the zoo on PAGE 55.

"A red-haired boy is visiting the space station," you tell the robot. "Can your machine find him?"

"Of course," the robot says, twisting some dials.

Denny's face ripples across the screen. He's crouched underneath a table that holds a large computer. As you stare at your brother you realize the table is in this very room!

"Denny!" you cry. You run towards the table. Denny is still huddled there, too scared to move or speak.

Swiftly, you duck past the robot and under the desk.

"No!" the robot cries, coming after you. But you grab your brother's hand, then press the top and bottom buttons on the chronometer. As Dr Peebles instructed, you hold them down for five seconds.

Travel to PAGE 75.

You roll right into the knight's path.

"EEEYOW!" the knight cries as you hit him hard. He falls over backwards, and Denny sails out of his arms.

Denny cries out as he hits the roof. But he immediately scrambles to his feet.

"Quick!" you tell Denny. "Untie my hands! We've got to get out of here!"

"You're not the boss of me!" Denny says. But for once he actually does what you say.

Now the knight is on his feet again, his eyes burning with rage.

"I'll destroy both of you!" he bellows. He lunges for you and your brother.

Quick! Grab the chronometer and press a button—any button! Then turn to PAGE 96.

You crawl through the small opening. In the darkness the red lights glitter like jewels.

Sticky, rope-like strands hang from the walls and ceiling. At the end of each strand there's a big grey lump.

You move closer to the strands and shudder.

The strands are part of a big spiderweb! And the big grey lumps are the bodies of giant insects!

"Help me!" a voice cries out.

As you stare at the web you realize one of the wrapped-up insects is much larger than the others.

"Help me!"

It's Denny! A giant spider has wrapped him up in its silk!

Quick! Turn to PAGE 39.

You take off after the knight on horseback. The enormous stone castle stretches towards the sky. Flags fly from its turrets.

You imagine living there. Cool! you think.

Suddenly you notice that the knight has disappeared. Where did he go?

You hurry over a drawbridge, which stretches over a moat. The moat surrounds the castle.

The sound of thundering hooves breaks the silence. The knight is returning, at full speed. And now he's holding a spear—and pointing it at you!

"Hey!" you call out. "I'm not your enemy! I'm a visitor from the future!"

But the knight doesn't pay attention. His horse gallops closer and closer. The tip of the knight's spear gleams in the sun.

Uh-oh. This guy looks pretty serious. Are you ready to face him? Or should you jump into the moat below, even though you're a terrible swimmer?

Face the knight on PAGE 22.
Jump into the moat on PAGE 108.

94

Quickly, you pull the chronometer from around your neck and put it in the keyhole.

"RRAAAOOORRRGGGHHH!" the dragon bellows, filling the small room with flames and more smoke.

The woman shrieks in terror. You turn the chronometer in the lock. To your surprise, the lock pops open. The woman quickly pulls off her chains, then grabs your hand. "This way!" she cries. "The dragon can't follow!"

She leads you through a small door and slams it. Behind the door, the dragon roars angrily.

"Thank you for saving me," the woman says. "Is there any way I can repay you?"

You explain that you're looking for your brother. "He has red hair," you say, describing him.

The woman nods. "I've seen a young boy who looks just like that in the Throne Room." She points to a door labelled TO KING RUTHBERT'S THRONE ROOM.

You glance at the chronometer. Time is running out! You've got only half an hour to find Denny and return to the present.

"Good luck." The woman smiles. "And thanks again."

Turn to PAGE 83.

You yank your hand away from the lion. To your surprise, it lets you go. But just as you are about to press the buttons on the chronometer, the lion pounces on your brother, knocking you both over.

The chronometer flies out of your hand. At the same moment, there's a loud *pop!* Denny disappears into the air. With a squeak of surprise, the lion disappears, too!

You look all around, but there's no sign of either your brother or the beast. And the chronometer lies smashed on the floor.

Oh, no! Now you've done it. Maybe the wizard can help you.

You wander back through the castle, trying to find the wizard's lair. At last you come to the door labelled: LAIR OF THE WIZARD.

See the wizard on PAGE 19.

You press the button under your middle finger and immediately feel a tingling sensation. When it stops, you're standing near small trees. In the distance long-necked dinosaurs are grazing on some plants.

While you're gazing at the dinosaurs, Denny says, "Look at these weird rocks!"

Denny's standing next to six round, speckled boulders. They're not rocks, you realize. They're eggs. Dinosaur eggs! As you stare at the rocks, you hear a steady tapping sound. Then one of them begins to crack.

"Wow!" you cry. "I think this egg's about to hatch!"

"I want to do something else," Denny whines. "I'm bored." He grabs the chronometer and runs off.

"Denny, come back!" you scream. But he keeps running.

You're going to have to go after him. But if you do, you'll miss the coolest thing that's happened since you got here. What should you do?

Watch the egg hatch on PAGE 130.
Chase Denny on PAGE 61.

The squealing of brakes fills the air. The lorry lurches to a stop right before your family.

CRASH!

A taxicab slams into the back of the lorry. Horns blare and several drivers jump from their cars as a horrible stench fills the air.

What's going on?

You leap out of the lorry and run around to the back. Luckily, the driver of the taxi is fine, but the lorry's back doors have been smashed in. And now a river of dead, slippery fish is flowing out of the back, on to the taxicab's hood, and into the street.

Yuk!

You grab the chronometer and push down on the buttons.

You're sorry about leaving Denny behind in the future, but, as he always says—you're not the boss of him.

THE END

The space shuttle finally docks at a huge, orbiting space station. The doors glide open. You walk off the shuttle and enter a corridor.

Inside the space station, robots and humans hurry along the walkway. Denny might be here somewhere—but where?

A pair of robots wearing security badges stare right at you. All the other humans are wearing bright yellow uniforms, you notice. You'd better find one right away, before someone tries to stop you.

Just ahead is a door marked SUPPLIES. Inside, a pile of freshly laundered uniforms sits on a shelf.

Put on the uniform and turn to PAGE 24.

You're sure you can trick the robot. After all, you're human and he's just a machine.

"Please don't shoot me," you cry. "I'm a visitor from the past. I'm only here to find my brother."

The robot hesitates. It seems to be computing what you just said. Then it pulls back the trigger on its laser.

"I could prove it if you had better technology," you add.

The robot's electronic eye flashes angrily. "Our technology has been perfected," it states.

"Too bad." You heave a big sigh. "I mean, you probably can't locate the time I left the present."

The robot scuttles over. "When did you leave?" it demands. "I can find that!"

You tell the robot the exact day and time that you left Dr Peebles's laboratory.

The robot adjusts some controls. Then Dr Peebles's laboratory appears on the large central monitor.

Watch what happens on PAGE 129.

100

You've got to get away from the fierce tyrannosaur. You grab Denny's hand and take off through the trees. The dinosaur chases you, but it's too big to fit easily between the trees.

You and Denny zig one way and zag another. Finally the two of you crouch down behind a thick tree trunk. You both gasp for air.

In the distance, you can see the tyrannosaur. It glances all around. At last it lets out a defeated-sounding roar and ambles off.

"Way to go!" Denny shouts. You and your brother high-five each other. Now all you have to do is go back to the swamp and find the chronometer.

But which direction is it? You've done so much twisting and turning, you aren't sure where the swamp is.

Luckily, Denny seems to remember the way. You follow him through the forest and finally come to the swampland. As you rush over to the pool of quicksand, all you can think about is the time ticking by. How much longer before Denny disappears for ever?

Turn to PAGE 12.

You decide to go towards the futuristic city. All around you are buildings made of shiny metal and glass. Cars—with wings—fly above your head. The streets are empty and clean, with no litter—not even a gum wrapper.

Is this New York in the future? It certainly looks different from the one you're visiting in the present.

You're about to start looking for Denny when a hand closes on your shoulder in an icy grip.

"Human?" a hollow-sounding voice says. "You're under arrest!"

You whirl around. Gripping your shoulder is a shiny metal robot with a policeman's badge welded to its chest. The robot's face is expressionless, and it's holding something that looks like a laser gun. No wonder everything is so clean and quiet, you think. The city is run by machines!

"Don't you know that humans aren't allowed out in the streets?" the robot demands.

"I come from . . . another place," you quickly reply. "I don't know your rules. Please give me another chance."

"That's for the judge to decide," the robot says. "Come with me."

Turn to Page 89.

102

"Look at this one!" says a little robot. It gazes at the sign in front of the force field. "It's the 'Couch Potato' exhibit," the small robot goes on. It begins making strange noises again.

"It's not polite to laugh at the humans," one of the bigger robots says.

"But Mummy," replies the little one. "It's so funny-looking. Here, human!" it adds. It shoves something through the force field. You lean down to pick up a chocolate bar.

"Look!" says the little one. "It picked up the chocolate! It's eating it!" The small robot pushes another chocolate bar through the force field.

With a sinking feeling, you realize that you're stuck here for good. But cheer up. At least when the little robots visit, you'll get to eat plenty of chocolate.

THE END

"The three objects are a pin, a pipe and a potato," you tell the robot.

"WRONG!" the teacher thunders. "You know the penalty for a *wrong* answer! Now step forward!"

You start towards the frammilizer. Slowly you feel for the chronometer around your neck. But before you can press any buttons, the robot snatches it away with its magnetic claws.

"No tricks!" the robot says. "Now enter the frammilizer!"

There's no way out now.

As you step into the strange metal box, your heart sinks to the bottom of your toes. You're a complete failure. You haven't found Denny, and you couldn't answer the teacher's question. Then again, you're about to become the first kid you know to be frammilized.

THE END

104

"Excuse me," you say, walking over to the lorry driver. "The dispatcher asked if you could take me on your delivery. My uncle owns the shop you're delivering to, and I need a lift there."

"Sure, kid," he says. "Why not?"

You follow him to the green lorry. He opens the back. Cases of fresh fish are piled inside. The dead fish stare at you with cold, empty eyes.

"Hop in," the driver says.

"In there? B-but . . ." you stammer.

"The cab's full," he says. "Do you want a lift or not?"

"Uh . . ." You really need to be in the front with him. But you don't know what else to do, so you climb into the back of the lorry and sit down.

When the driver shuts the door, everything goes dark. You can't believe how bad it smells back here. And the fishes' cold, scaly bodies keep brushing against you.

Yuck!

Hold your nose and turn to PAGE 27.

As the lorry bears down on your family, the driver seems totally paralysed. In fact, he seems to have fainted!

You struggle out of your seat belt. It's up to you to do something!

This is what you planned for.

This is why you came back to this time. But somehow you didn't think it would be so hard to stop the lorry.

Maybe you can steer the lorry on to another street. Or should you try to reach the brakes?

Make a decision quick!

Try to steer the lorry? Turn to PAGE 13.
Go for the brakes? Turn to PAGE 67.

You hold your breath and brace yourself as you fall towards the bubbling pot.

You pull your arms into your chest. And your hand hits a button. A button on the chronometer!

Your body begins to tingle. You close your eyes and cross your fingers. And then you land.

But not in bubbling oil!

Blinking, you gaze around. You're in a room. Dr Peebles's lab. You made it back to the present!

"Welcome, time traveller!" Dr Peebles greets you. "How did it go?"

You're about to answer when you remember Denny. Oh, no! You left Denny in the past.

"I've got to save my brother—" you start to say. And then you remember the pot of oil. The *boiling* oil. A lot Denny did for me when I was about to be fried! you think.

"Excellent!" you say to Dr Peebles. "Everything was excellent."

Then you head back towards the museum exhibits. Of course, now you have to explain to your parents why their youngest son is now called Ruthelford and lives in medieval times!

THE END

Yes! The door of the lorry opens. There's Abe, looking absolutely shocked as mice scamper out of the lorry and all over the loading dock.

"Hey you," you hear Abe call to the driver of the green lorry. "Get out that lorry and help us clear up this mess."

Congratulations, time traveller. The truck drivers are so busy chasing white mice that the green lorry doesn't get to the intersection until way after your family is out of there.

You did it! You're a hero. You saved your family. And you saved the lives of two thousand white mice.

THE END

You decide to take your chances in the moat.

SPLASH! The water is cold—but at least you escaped that fierce-looking knight.

Then you hear it—a loud clacking sound.

A crocodile snapping his jaws. He's right in front of you! And he looks mighty hungry!

You turn away from the crocodile and swim in the opposite direction. You wish you could swim faster. The crocodile's gaining on you!

Suddenly another crocodile pops up in your path. And another.

You're totally surrounded by hungry green crocodiles!

You grab for the chronometer around your neck. But before you can press the buttons, the crocodile nearest to you snatches it out of your hand.

In one gulp, he swallows it!

Too bad. The chronometer was only the appetizer. The main course is about to be served—and it's you!

THE END

You listen as Jarmal explains about the rebellion.

"The robots were originally created by humans as servants. But gradually their powers grew greater and greater. Eventually, they took over."

"So now the humans are fighting back?" you ask.

"Exactly," Jarmal says. "We expect the battle to begin any minute. We—"

BOOM! His words are cut off by a deafening blast.

The battle begins on PAGE 10.

110

You reach the swamp and grab Denny's hands. With all your might, you pull. But Denny is completely stuck!

You pull Denny again. This time he panics. He grabs wildly at you. The chronometer flies off the chain around your neck and into the mud.

Now the tyrannosaur is only a few yards away. Its terrible face is so close, you can see its sharp, pointed teeth and smell its hot, stinking breath. The dinosaur roars, shaking the nearby trees.

You yank Denny one more time. With a loud *plop!* he's freed from the quicksand. But now the tyrannosaur is only a few feet away. It opens its mouth wide and stretches its fierce claws towards you.

Frantically, you look around for the chronometer. You've got to get back to the present. But there's no trace of the stopwatch. It's been sucked into the mud!

Should you try to dig the chronometer out of the muck? Or try to run away from the tyrannosaur? Which will you choose?

If you decide to dig for the chronometer, turn to PAGE 126.

Think you can escape the tyrannosaur? Turn to PAGE 100.

"Welcome to the rebel forces!" Jarmal cries, shaking your hand. He shows you a map of The City and explains the battle plan. "This building beams power to all the robots," he says, pointing to a large plant on the map. "If we can blow up this power plant, the robots will become helpless."

Next, Jarmal shows you a small, red box. "This box contains a special explosive," he explains. "It must be placed within three feet of the power source."

You follow Jarmal through the tunnel to a stairway leading to a park. Through the trees you see the power plant. It's a tall, white, completely round building with a large antenna extending from the roof.

Jarmal tells you that all entrances are heavily guarded by robots. "Since none of the robots will recognize you, you've been chosen to enter the power plant," he says.

"What?" you exclaim. "You want *me* to enter the power plant?"

"Didn't I mention it before?" asks Jarmal. "Our entire plan depends on you. Are you ready?"

Are you? Then turn to PAGE 119.

112

"It is a great honour for a human to be accepted into the college." The robot leads you out of the plant to a small flying car. "And you know what happens to humans who turn down robot honours."

You don't know—but you can guess.

The car lands on top of a tall brick building.

"Your lecture hall is right this way," the robot tells you.

"I need time to prepare—" you start to say.

"Nonsense," the robot cuts you off. "A good teacher doesn't need preparation."

The next thing you know, you're facing a large classroom full of shiny metal robots. They all have portable computers in front of them, ready to take notes.

Maybe, just maybe, the rebels will manage to free The City and help you and Denny get out of the future.

In the meantime, you cross your fingers and start to tell the robots everything you've ever known about snazzilizers and romiframptons.

THE END

You crouch down and open the foot-high wooden door to the Lair of the Lizard. You can't see anything but darkness. You hold your breath to make yourself smaller, then wriggle through the door on your stomach.

Inside, you stand up. You're in a dark, misty room. Flies and other insects dart from wall to wall.

A bearded man in flowing robes bursts into the room from another door. He peers through the mist. "Wizard!" he calls. "Wizard! Where are you?"

"Excuse me?" you say politely. "Aren't you the wizard?"

"Of course I am!" he bellows. "I'm the wizard, but I can't find my lizard named Wizard. Have you seen him?"

"No," you say, "but I'm looking for someone, too. I—"

"I know who you are and what you seek," he interrupts. "You are a traveller in time."

"Yes," you tell him, surprised. "And I'm looking—"

"The young boy you seek is lost in the Corridors of Time," he says. "To find him, you must answer a question of time."

At the mention of time, you glance at the chronometer. Time is running out!

To answer the question, hurry to PAGE 33.

114

"Denny!" you cry. "Come back!"

You run to the back of the Lair. Denny is slipping into a small, dark opening between two bookcases.

Inside the opening you can hear heavy breathing. It doesn't sound human!

Do you still have the nerve to follow Denny?

If so, turn to PAGE 45.

"Human spies!" the robot with the laser gun declares. "You are under arrest!"

You untwist yourself and float out of the chamber. "We weren't spying!" you protest. "We were only—"

"Silence!" the robot snaps.

In a panic, you pull out the chronometer and take a glance. You and Denny have to get home.

"Please," you beg the robot. "I have to get my brother—"

"Explain it to the captain!" the robot says. It snatches away the chronometer.

"No!" you scream. "Give that back!" You grab for the chronometer, but the robot holds it beyond your reach. "Come along now!" it snarls. It clamps its metal claws around your wrist. "You, too!" it adds, reaching for Denny.

"You can't make me!" Denny kicks the robot hard on its metal shin and takes off running.

The robot stops for a moment. You can hear something whirring inside its head. "The captain will explain what to do," it mutters. "Now come with me."

Turn to PAGE 131.

116

"I'm ready to begin the duel," the knight tells you. He plucks an apple from the tree. Then he winds up and throws the apple towards you. Holding the club like a baseball bat, you smack the apple. It soars down the path, past the knight.

"I can hit it much further," the knight boasts. He takes his place at the end of the drawbridge.

Now you pick an apple from the tree. You stand on the pitcher's mound and eye the knight. Then you wind up. You pitch.

The knight swings with all his might.

And hits a blooper a few feet in front of you.

All right!

"I won," you call. "Now can I go into the castle? I need to look for my brother."

The knight nods. "Very well, stranger," he says sadly. "You may enter the castle. But according to the rules, I must jump into the moat."

Go to PAGE 50.

You'd like to help the woman, but it's more important to find Denny. You race out of the smoky room.

"Halt!" the woman screams. "You've failed the knight test!"

"What?"

"I'm not really a helpless maiden," the woman explains. She breaks free of the chains holding her to the wall. "I'm actually the dragon's keeper. This is a test we set up for future knights. Anyone who refuses to try to rescue the maiden fails."

"But I don't want to be a knight!" you protest.

"Of course you do," says the maiden. "Otherwise, why would you be in this room?"

"I'm looking for my brother—" you start to say, but it's no use.

The maiden snaps her finger, and the dragon slithers into the room towards you!

Turn to PAGE 8.

118

You set out along the walkway, searching for the power source. You come to a large platform guarded by a robot.

"Halt, human!" it demands. "What is your business here?"

"I'm here to fix the romiframpton," you tell the robot.

"What's wrong with it?" the robot demands.

You think quickly, then say the first thing that comes to your mind. "The snazzilizer is pulsing out of phase."

"No wonder it's been so scaloopy lately," the robot replies. "You're the first entity—robot or human—to diagnose the problem correctly."

The robot actually believed you! You're in shock, and it takes you a minute to speak.

". . . I'd better get to work," you say finally.

"Never mind the romiframpton," the robot says. "Now that we know what's wrong, we can fix it ourselves. But with your mechanical genius we can use you as an instructor in the electronics college. Come with me."

"No," you protest. "I need to—"

"I said, come with me!" the robot repeats in a nasty metallic twang.

Go to college on PAGE 112.

"No way," you protest. "I'm not going in there."

"If you want help finding your brother," Jarmal snaps, "you'd better do it."

Finally you agree. What else can you do?

Jarmal hands you the red box with the explosives. "Remember, you have to place it within three feet of the power source. And one more thing . . . you have only one minute to get away before it blows."

"How am I supposed to get into the building?" you ask.

"There are two ways to get in," Jarmal tells you. "One is to find some way to get past the robot guards at the door."

"No thanks," you mutter. "What's the other way?"

"You could crawl in through the air duct," Jarmal says. "That way you'll avoid the robots— but the ducts are very narrow. Crawling through them could be very, very dangerous."

How will you enter the building?

Decide carefully—the fate of humans on Earth may depend on your answer!

Try to fool the guards? Turn to PAGE 29.

Crawl in through the air duct? Turn to PAGE 79.

120

You decide to try the truth.

"I'm not a spy," you repeat. "But I'm not a crew member either. I'm actually a time traveller."

"Likely story!" the captain snarls. "If you're a time traveller, prove it!"

"The device your guard took from me is a chronometer," you explain. "That's how I move from one time to another."

The guard hands the chronometer to the captain. She glances at it, then hands it back to you. You quickly slip it under your uniform in case she changes her mind.

"If you are really from the past," she says to you, "what colour were the eyes of an allosaurus?"

"I'm not from *that* far back," you protest.

She sighs. "Okay, while I decide what to do with you, wait outside."

The guards each take one of your arms and roughly shove you out into the corridor.

Turn to PAGE 69.

Denny screams in terror as the knight prepares to toss him to the ground.

"Stop!" you yell. "That's King Ruthbert's son, Ruthelford," you say.

The knight looks at you in surprise. "Of course. Why do you think I'm getting ready to dash his brains out?"

"King Ruthbert will pay a huge ransom for him," you go on. "More gold and jewels than you can imagine."

"Is that right?" the knight replies. "How do you know?"

"I'm an agent of the king," you tell the knight. It's the first lie that enters your mind.

"Really? Then why are your hands tied?" the knight asks.

"Well, uh, er . . ." You try to think of a good answer. "Untie me and I'll show you!"

The knight looks you up and down. He draws his sword.

Oh, no! What's he going to do?

Got to PAGE 88.

122

You reach out to grab Denny before hitting the buttons on the chronometer.

"NOOO!" Denny shrieks. He pulls away and tears off down the street.

"Denny, come back here!" you yell. But Denny keeps going. He darts across the street and runs smack into his double—the future Denny. They both fall on to the pavement.

Your mother's face goes white when she sees two Dennys.

"Okay," your father demands. "Which one of you is really my son?"

"I am!" says one of the red-haired Dennys.

"*I* am," insists the other one. He punches the first one on the arm. The other Denny punches back.

You've got to do something! You rush across the street and grab both Dennys. Then you push the buttons on the chronometer.

Travel back to the present on PAGE 66.

You grab the rake. Then, holding it out in front of you, you inch towards the door on the other side of the room. The vine follows you, its flower head still snapping like mad.

You're about to reach for the doorknob when something grabs your ankle.

The vine is coiling around your legs!

Desperately, you hack at the vine with the rake. But it's no use. The vine rapidly works its way up your body, wrapping you up as tightly as a mummy!

Suddenly the door opens. Someone walks in, singing the words to your favourite song.

It's Denny!

You open your mouth to yell to him. But it's no use. You can't speak—you can't even move.

You hear Denny moving around the room, looking at everything. Then he stops right in front of you.

He looks closely at the vine holding you prisoner. "Cool plant," he says.

Cool plant?

That's not a plant—it's you!

THE END

124

You ask someone to point out the driver of the green lorry. He's a grey-haired man in a plaid jacket.

Now you have to decide what to say to him. Maybe you can get him to take you along with him, and then, at the crucial moment, you can steer the lorry away from your family.

Finally, you come up with two plans. You could tell him you're from out of town and you're lost, and you want a lift to your hotel. Or you could pretend the dispatcher wants him to take you along on the next delivery.

Which will you choose?

Tell the driver you're lost on PAGE 26.
Pretend the dispatcher sent you on PAGE 104.

"Please help me!" you beg the robot. "I'm looking for my brother and—"

"Silence, intruder," the robot commands. Keeping its laser trained on you, it waves you over to a chair in front of one of the monitors.

"You will be my helper in the Teletime room, human. I need someone to help me study the past," the robot explains. It points to one of the monitors. "You will watch this screen all night and all day and report to me on what you see."

That's not bad, you think. At least I'll get to watch TV!

You settle into one of the cushioned chairs opposite the monitor. On the screen, George Washington is crossing the Delaware River. You watch him do it again.

And again.

It's interesting the first few times, but after that you get bored. *Really* bored.

The days, months and finally years slowly pass. George is still crossing the river. And you're still watching.

Compared to this non-stop history lesson, going to museums with your parents was a total blast!

THE END

126

You've got to find the chronometer. You stick your arm deep into the quicksand. You feel around with your fingers . . . nothing.

Suddenly the *Tyrannosaurus rex* lets out a roar.

You plunge both hands into the quicksand. Beside you, Denny drops to his hands and knees to search, too.

You sift frantically through the mud. The dinosaur comes closer and closer. He reaches out one claw. Then he lets out a tremendous sound. It's a burp from his earlier feast—a gigantic burp as loud as an explosion!

The force of the burp knocks both you and Denny over. The two of you pitch forward . . . right into the quicksand!

Oh, no! You're both being pulled down, down into the quivering muck, to meet . . .

THE END

You decide to try to get back to Dr Peebles's lab. But is there enough time?

The student in front of you has given a wrong answer.

"No!" the girl cries. "Give me another chance!" But the teacher shoves the student into the frammilizer. And now the robot's red electronic eye fixes on *you*.

"How many electrons can be found in a pound of toffee?" the teacher asks you.

You grasp the chronometer and place your fingers over the top and bottom buttons to return to Dr Peebles's laboratory.

"Answer!" the robot thunders.

You quickly press the buttons.

SPROIINNGGG! There is a hideous sound as the chronometer disintegrates in your hand. Tiny wheels and computer chips fly all over your desk.

"Answer the question!" the robot repeats.

Too bad. There's no way you can return to your time. But cheer up—unless you know the answer to the question, you won't have to stay in the classroom very long!

THE END

128

You start up the metallic ladder, making sure that the red box is still inside your pocket. The building is at least thirty storeys high. At the top of the steps is a pulsing green glow.

The power source, you realize.

You climb faster. Soon you are at the top of the ladder, staring at a huge, green-glowing orb inside a round room with glass panels.

The glow is so bright you can hardly see. You look for a way into the room and finally notice a small door with a sign: EXTREME DANGER. DO NOT ENTER.

But you have to enter, to leave the explosive device.

Or do you?

Jarmal said only that the explosive device needed to be within three feet of the power source. He never said it had to be in the same room. Maybe you're already close enough.

Decide what to do right away—a robot guard is coming!

To enter the room, turn to PAGE 42.

Or to place the device against the wall and see what happens, turn to PAGE 49.

All right! The robot fell for it!

You can see yourself stepping into the Chronoport. Then you hear Dr Peebles say: "One more thing! Remember to hold the buttons down for at least five seconds!"

That's exactly what you needed to hear. Now you know how to make the chronometer work! But you still can't find Denny.

"I don't believe your Teletime machine really shows the past," you say.

"What!!??" the robot roars. "How dare you insult my machine!" Its finger moves closer to the trigger.

"If it really works," you say quickly, "then show me the present."

"The present?" the robot cries.

"Yes!" You nod. "The scenes from the past could have been films or videotapes. If I see scenes from the present, I'll believe the machine really works."

"Very well," the robot grumbles. "But right afterwards I will take pleasure in vaporizing you. Any particular scene in the present?" it adds sarcastically.

You smile. Your plan is working.

Turn to PAGE 90.

130

No way. You're not going to miss seeing a real dinosaur being born. You'll catch up with Denny in a few minutes.

You keep your eyes on the big speckled egg.

This is too cool, you think. Maybe it's a brachiosaurus or a triceratops. You've always wanted to see one of them.

Tap. Tap. Tap.

The baby dinosaur struggles to get out.

CRACK! The enormous egg splits open.

You lean forward—you're dying to see this!

Then out it pops. You see a long tail . . . a tiny beak . . . and soft wet feathers.

FEATHERS?

You can't believe it. This baby's not a dinosaur. It's a chicken.

Some kind of weird, prehistoric chicken!

Okay. Now you've learned your lesson.

Never count your dinosaurs before they hatch!

THE END

You follow the robot to meet the captain.

The captain of the ship is a woman. A human woman—but she looks really mean.

"You were caught spying in our secret anti-gravity device," she says sternly. "The penalty is immediate execution. Now what do you have to say for yourself?"

Immediate execution!

Somehow, you have to get her to understand what you were doing there. But what if she doesn't believe your story? Maybe it would be better to pretend you're a new member of the space crew and didn't know better.

Decide well. Your life depends on it!

Lie? Turn to PAGE 25.
Tell the truth? Go to PAGE 120.

"You're not the boss of me!" Denny says again. "Go ahead, Dad!"

"Prepare to boil, spy!" the knight on your right side snarls. He starts to drag you to the edge of the platform.

"Wait!" you cry. You look at the king. "Before you carry out the sentence, I have something that belongs to your son."

"Halt!" the king commands. "What is it?"

"A valuable piece of jewellery," you say. "Please allow me to give it to him."

"Yeah!" Denny says. "Give it to me!"

Turn to PAGE 14.

The teacher turns to you. "Stand up," the robot orders.

Nervously, you stand. You hold your breath as the teacher starts to speak. This is the moment. Can you answer the question, or will you be frammilized?

"The ancient British wizard Morgred used a magic spell to travel in time. The spell made use of three magical objects. What are they?"

Morgred? He was the wizard in the GOOSEBUMPS book *A Night in Terror Tower*. You remember him. But can you remember the answer to the question? If you can't, you'll have to guess! Think carefully, then answer.

Are the three objects a pin, a pipe and a potato? If so, turn to PAGE 103.

Or are the magical objects three white stones? If that is your answer, turn to PAGE 28.

Somehow you've got to talk Denny into coming back to the present with you. But how?

Then you get an idea. "Denny," you say very calmly. "I'm going back to Dr Peebles's laboratory now. But I don't want you to come with me."

"Why not?" Denny asks suspiciously.

"It's none of your business," you say as nastily as you can. "You can come back later today—or tomorrow."

"No!" Denny whines. "I want to go back *now*."

"Well, you can't," you say. "I'm going without you."

"NOOOO!" he whines louder. "Take me with you!"

"Sorry."

"I'll tell Mum!" he insists. "I'll tell her how you're always trying to be the boss of me."

"Oh, all right," you say, trying to sound disgusted. "Hold my hand, then." Looking pleased, Denny takes your hand. You glance down at the chronometer. Forty-five seconds—plenty of time to spare. And Denny doesn't even realize that he tricked himself!

THE END

Mice! The boxes are full of mice. White mice to be used at the lab for research.

Looking at the mice gives you an idea.

As fast as you can, you start opening the boxes and releasing the mice. Before you know it, there are mice all over the lorry.

"Help! Help!" you scream, banging on the back of the lorry.

Will anyone hear you?

Turn to PAGE 107.

R.L.Stine

Reader beware, you're in for a scare!
These terrifying tales will send shivers up your spine:

Reader beware – you choose the scare!

A scary new series from R.L. Stine – where *you* decide what happens!

Give Yourself Goosebumps 1:
Escape From the Carnival of Horrors

Late one night you and your friends decide to visit the annual
carnival. It's not open yet, but you sneak in
anyway. *Big* mistake. Because sneaking out again
might not be so easy…

Pick one ending and you'll all ride on the deadly Doom Slide
till the end of time. Select another, and you'll be trapped in a
freak show … for ever. So be careful how you choose your
rides … and your endings!

Reader beware – here's THREE TIMES the scare!

Look out for these bumper GOOSEBUMPS editions. With three spine-tingling stories by R.L. Stine in each book, get ready for three times the thrill … three times the scare … three times the GOOSEBUMPS!

GOOSEBUMPS COLLECTION 1
Welcome to Dead House
Say Cheese and Die
Stay Out of the Basement

GOOSEBUMPS COLLECTION 2
The Curse of the Mummy's Tomb
Let's Get Invisible!
Night of the Living Dummy

GOOSEBUMPS COLLECTION 3
The Girl Who Cried Monster
Welcome to Camp Nightmare
The Ghost Next Door

GOOSEBUMPS COLLECTION 4
The Haunted Mask
Piano Lessons Can Be Murder

Goosebumps

Reader beware – we're counting down to a scare!

THREE completely new Goosebumps titles in one book…

TWO hard covers which make it the first EVER Goosebumps hardback…

ONE weird wailing chip that'll make you jump out of your skin…

LIFT-OFF! It's the **GOOSEBUMPS WAILING SPECIAL**, blasting into a bookshop near you. Don't be the only one to miss take-off…